BLACKBERRY FARM

LUCY MOUSE KEEPS A SECRET

Jane Pilgrim

This edition first published in the United Kingdom in 1999 by
Brockhampton Press
20 Bloomsbury Street
London WC1B 3QA
a member of the Hodder Headline PLC Group

Designed and Produced for Brockhampton Press by
Open Door Limited
80 High Street, Colsterworth, Lincolnshire, NG33 5JA

Illustrator: F. Stocks May
Colour separation: GA Graphics Stamford

Title: BLACKBERRY FARM, Lucy Mouse Keeps a Secret
ISBN: 1-84186-003-4

LUCY MOUSE KEEPS A SECRET

Jane Pilgrim

Illustrated by F. Stocks May

BROCKHAMPTON PRESS

Lucy Mouse had always lived at Blackberry Farm. She was born in a corner of the old stable, and lived there with her mother and father and two little sisters and three little brothers. She was a quiet, kind, brown mouse, and was always ready to help anyone.

Mrs Nibble, who lived with her
family in a little house in the bank
of the field below Blackberry
Farm, was a great friend of Lucy
Mouse. And Lucy often went down
to see her and to help her with her
three bunnies, Rosy, Posy and
Christopher.

One day when Lucy was crossing the yard on her way to see Mrs Nibble she saw a strange brown mouse sitting on a stone by the gate. He smiled politely at her as she went past.

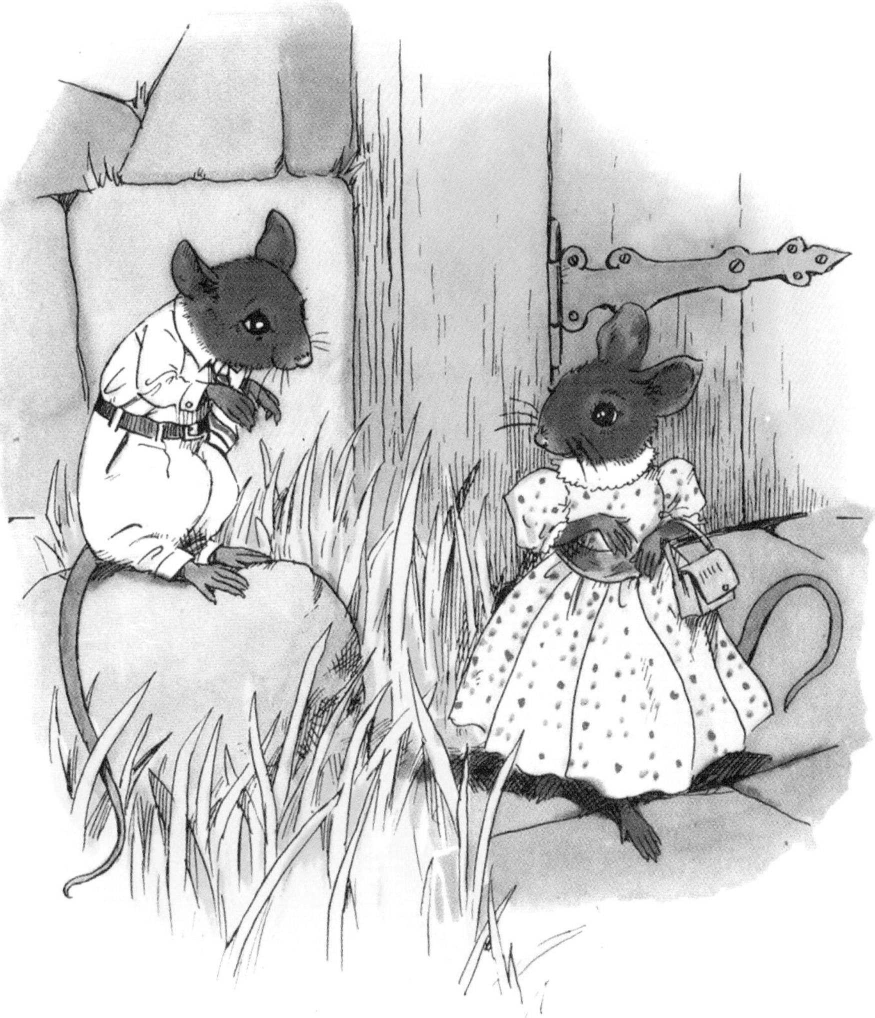

The next day he was there again,
and the next day, and the next
day, and the next day. Each time
he just smiled at Lucy, but on
the ninth day he jumped off his
stone and walked beside her into
the field.

Now Joe Robin had been
watching all this, and he flew over
to see Mrs Nibble. "Who is the
strange brown mouse whom Lucy
is meeting?" he asked her. "I
haven't seen him at Blackberry
Farm before." But Mrs Nibble did
not know. "I will ask Lucy next
time she comes to see me,"
she said.

But Lucy did not got to see Mrs
Nibble again, because she was too
busy walking in the field with the
strange brown mouse.

One day Emily the Goat found Lucy busy in a corner of her stable. She had a brush and a dustpan and was sweeping it very clean. "Why are you doing that, Lucy?" Emily asked. But Lucy just smiled and went on sweeping.

Then Walter Duck met her carrying some corn out of the barn. "What are you going to do with that, Lucy?" he asked. But Lucy just smiled and hurried over to Emily's stable.

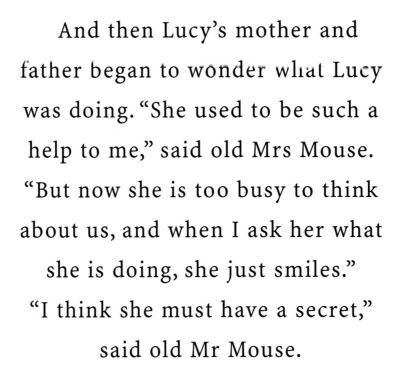

And then Lucy's mother and father began to wonder what Lucy was doing. "She used to be such a help to me," said old Mrs Mouse. "But now she is too busy to think about us, and when I ask her what she is doing, she just smiles."

"I think she must have a secret," said old Mr Mouse.

And all Blackberry Farm began
to talk about Lucy Mouse's secret.
But Lucy Mouse just went on
smiling and being busy and
going for walks with the strange
brown mouse.

Then one sunny morning there was a knock on Mrs Nibble's door, and when she opened it she saw Lucy and the strange brown mouse standing together on her doorstep. "I want you to meet my friend Marcus," Lucy said. "He lives down the lane at Oakapple Cottage, and I hope he will soon live at Blackberry Farm."
Mrs Nibble shook hands with Marcus, and said she was very glad to meet him.

The next day Lucy took Marcus
to see her family. Marcus had a
long talk with old Mr Mouse, and
all Lucy's brothers and sisters
peeped out at him from under the
straw in the stable until old Mrs
Mouse shooed them away.

By now all the animals at the farm were very excited. "Tell us your secret, Lucy," they cried, as she walked towards the field with the strange brown mouse. But she just smiled and went on walking.

But Marcus, the strange brown mouse, stopped. "I will tell you Lucy's secret," he said. "She is going to marry me, and we are going to live in the corner of Emily's stable. I am a very proud and happy mouse."

Then all the animals shouted for joy, because they loved Lucy Mouse and were glad to see her so happy. "Three cheers for Lucy and Marcus," called Joe Robin. "And may they live happily ever afterwards at Blackberry Farm." And Lucy and Marcus smiled and waved, and everyone was happy with them.